Dinnertin Rhyme

Written by June Crebbin
Illustrated by Ana Martín Larrañaga

WALKER BOOKS
AND SUBSIDIARIES

LONDON • BOSTON • SYDNEY

Can you tell me,
if you please,
Who it is likes
squidgy peas?

Louise likes peas.

How about Jake?
Jake likes cake.

How about Ellen?
Ellen likes melon.

How about Trish?
Trish likes fish.

How about Fred?
Fred likes bread.

How about Hetty?
Hetty likes spaghetti.

How about Greg?
Greg likes egg.

How about Sam?
Sam likes jam.

OK then, tell me,
if you can –

how about
Katerina
Wilhelmina
Theodora
Dobson?

She likes –

jam
egg
spaghetti
bread
fish
melon
cake
peas
and ...

smelly
cheese!

For Nat
J.C.
For Rosario
A.M.L.

First published 2001 by Walker Books Ltd
87 Vauxhall Walk, London SE11 5HJ

2 4 6 8 10 9 7 5 3

Text © 2001 June Crebbin
Illustrations © 2001 Ana Martín Larrañaga

This book has been typeset in Avant Garde

Printed in Hong Kong

British Library Cataloguing in Publication Data:
a catalogue record for this book
is available from the British Library

ISBN 0-7445-8307-1